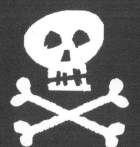
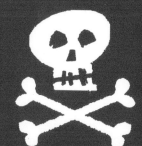

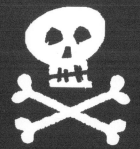
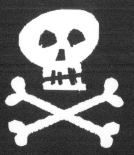

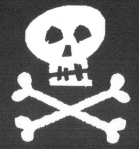

This Orchard book

belongs to

....

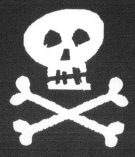

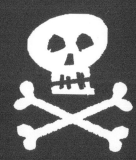
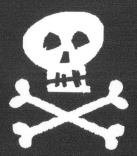
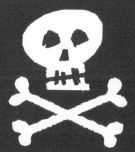
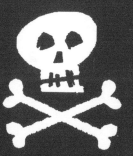

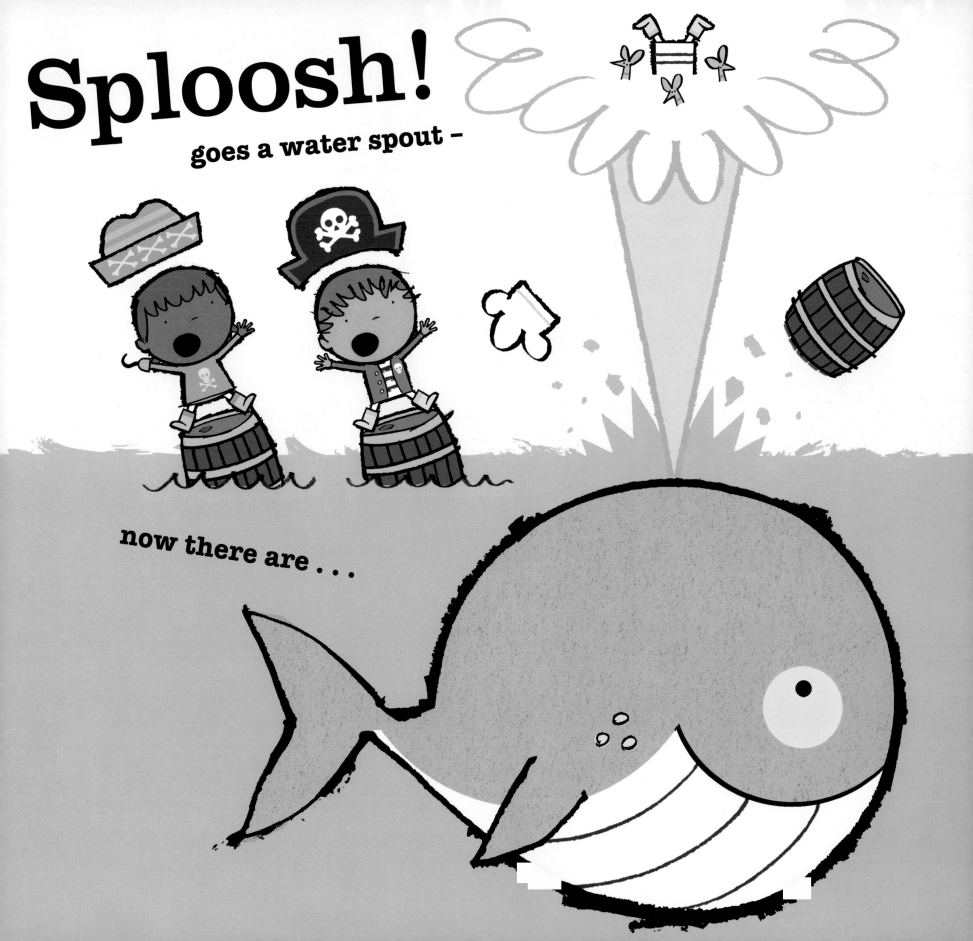

Sploosh!

goes a water spout –

now there are . . .

. . . two.

Two little pirates, baking in the sun.

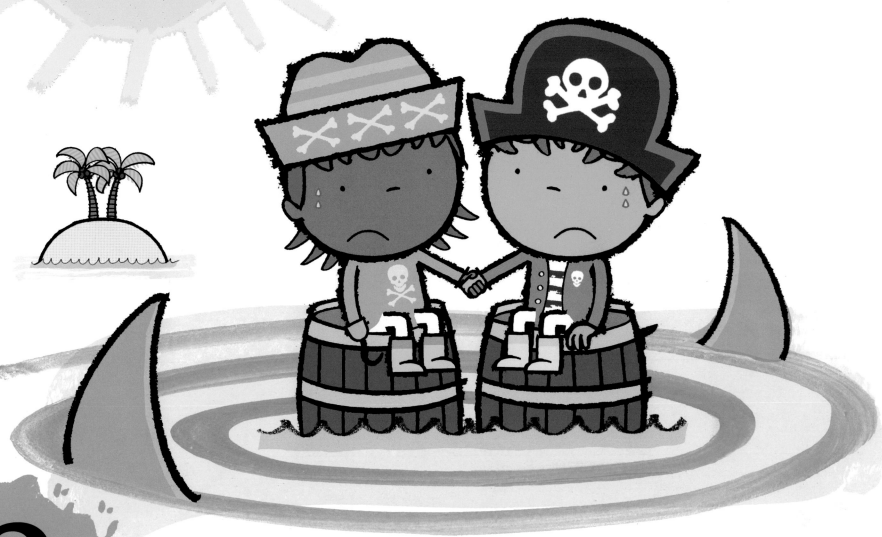

2

Snap!

goes a hungry shark –

now there is . . .